P9-CKY-679

The Kingdom
The Palace
Burth
Mermaid's Cove
Crestwood

of Wrenly
Flatfrost
Primlox
Bogburp
The Mainland
Hobsgrove

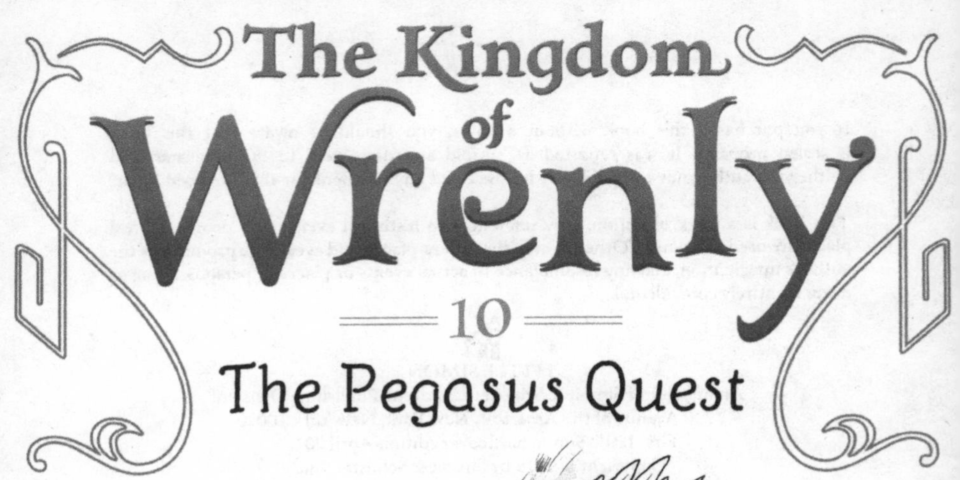

The Kingdom of Wrenly

10

The Pegasus Quest

By Jordan Quinn
Illustrated by Robert McPhillips

LITTLE SIMON
New York London Toronto Sydney New Delhi

LITTLE SIMON
An imprint of Simon & Schuster Children's Publishing Division
1230 Avenue of the Americas, New York, New York 10020
First Little Simon hardcover edition April 2016

Also available in a Little Simon paperback edition.

For information about special discounts for bulk purchases, please contact Simon & Schuster Special Sales at 1-866-506-1949 or business@simonandschuster.com.
The Simon & Schuster Speakers Bureau can bring authors to your live event. For more information or to book an event contact the Simon & Schuster Speakers Bureau at 1-866-248-3049 or visit our website at www.simonspeakers.com.
Designed by Laura Roode
Manufactured in the United States of America 0920 SKY
4 6 8 10 9 7 5 3
Library of Congress Cataloging-in-Publication Data
Quinn, Jordan.
The Pegasus quest / by Jordan Quinn ; illustrated by Robert McPhillips. —
First Little Simon hardcover edition.
pages cm. — (The Kingdom of Wrenly ; 10)
Summary: "As Lucas and Clara set out to investigate some mysterious happenings in Wrenly, they discover a young horse with wings that is lost and in danger"— Provided by publisher.
ISBN 978-1-4814-5871-9 (hc) — ISBN 978-1-4814-5870-2 (pbk) —
ISBN 978-1-4814-5872-6 (eBook) [1. Animals, Mythical—Fiction. 2. Princes—Fiction.]
I. McPhillips, Robert, illustrator. II. Title.
PZ7.Q31945Pe 2016
[Fic]—dc23
2015018537

CONTENTS

CHAPTER 1

Song of the Owls

Prince Lucas and his best friend, Clara Gills, leaned on the balcony railing and gazed at the full moon. A ribbon of blue light shimmered across the Sea of Wrenly. But this was no ordinary moon. It was a *blue* moon—something so rare it is said to happen only once in a lifetime. All the owls in the kingdom flocked together and sang once in a blue moon. Lucas and Clara waited and listened for the owl song.

Ruskin yawned, stretched, and curled up near the children. The young scarlet dragon had no interest in singing owls. He shut his eyes and sighed peacefully.

"Look at that enormous blue cloud," said Clara, pointing.

Lucas tilted his head back. "It's been there since this afternoon," he said.

"I know," Clara said, studying the cloud. "It hasn't budged."

Lucas looked at the great cloud

thoughtfully. "Maybe there's a floating castle inside it," he said.

Clara laughed. "You read too many fairy tales!" she said jokingly.

"And most of them have turned out to be true," Lucas reminded her.

Clara shook her head. "You're such a dreamer."

Then they began to hear a steady thrum. It sounded like the deep beating of wings. The friends turned toward the blue moon and gasped in wonder. Hundreds of owls swirled across the moonlight.

The children stood very still and listened. The owl song began softly, and gradually got louder.

Hoo Ha HOO-hoo-hoo! Hoo Ha HOO-hoo-hoo!

Goose bumps tingled and swept over the children.

"Listen," whispered Lucas. "They sound so spooky."

"Like a ghostly chorus," agreed Clara.

The owls sang and soared gracefully, round and round in the blue-glowing night sky.

"Wow, I wish I could fly like an owl," Lucas said, spreading his arms out.

"Me too," said Clara. "If I had

wings, I'd fly right up to that cloud."

The owls finished their eerie song and disappeared into the night. Then a dazzling shooting star blazed across the sky.

"Make a wish!" Lucas exclaimed.

The star left a sparkling trail of light as it vanished over Burth, the island of the trolls.

"What did you wish for?" asked Clara.

"I wished for an adventure," Lucas said.

"Me too," said Clara.

CHAPTER 2

Troubled Trolls

The next morning Lucas returned to the balcony with Ruskin. He noticed that the great cloud was still there. He wondered again about floating castles. Then he shook his head. He was about to go back inside, when he heard a few knights talking down below. He stood still and listened.

"The trolls are in an *uproar,*" he heard one of the knights declare.

"What seems to be the trouble?" asked another.

Lucas leaned against the railing. "Their prized ender-berry crop has been nearly wiped out," said the first knight.

The second knight gasped. "By what?"

"Nobody knows," the first knight replied. "We should investigate."

Lucas cupped his hand over his mouth. *Oh no!* he thought. *I have to tell Clara about this!*

The prince and Ruskin hurried over to Clara's house and told her what they had heard. Clara put down the broom in her hand.

"What are we waiting for?" she asked.

They ran down the hill and over the long stone bridge to Burth. All of the enderberry bushes grew in the meadows just over the bridge.

Lucas, Clara, and Ruskin slipped into the enderberry grove and began to inspect the bushes for clues. All they found were clusters of empty stems. Bush after bush had been picked clean of berries.

"Someone or something sure was hungry," said Lucas.

Clara shifted some branches and peeked deeper into the bush.

"There isn't a single berry in here!" she exclaimed.

Then they heard a rustle in the bushes.

Ruskin squawked.

"Get away from my bushes!"

boomed a gruff voice behind them.

Lucas, Clara, and Ruskin whirled around and came face-to-face with a grim-looking troll. But the troll's expression quickly changed when he saw it was the prince. He bowed.

"I beg your pardon, Your Majesty," the troll said. "I didn't know it was you!"

Then the troll introduced himself as Grumblesnout.

Lucas and Clara forgave the troll and apologized for their surprise visit.

"We're trying to figure out what

happened to your enderberries," said Clara.

Grumblesnout sighed heavily. "It's very mysterious," he said darkly. "You see, most creatures don't like the taste of enderberries. They are incredibly bitter and sour. But we trolls love them—though we can only eat a handful without sugar."

Lucas nodded. "Do you mind if we help look for clues?"

"Of course not," Grumblesnout said. "We need all the help we can get."

So Lucas and Clara began to look for animal tracks in and around the berryless bushes. Ruskin followed

behind, sniffing the ground for unusual scents. But they found nothing out of the ordinary. Then Lucas saw Grumblesnout across the field, talking with somebody.

"I wonder who that is?" questioned Lucas.

Clara looked over to see someone dressed in a brown hooded robe. The stranger had a lasso strapped to a belt, and a bow with arrows slung over one shoulder.

"I wonder if that stranger knows about the missing enderberries!" said Clara suspiciously.

"Let's find out!" Lucas said.

The children ran across the field toward Grumblesnout. But by

the time they reached the troll, the stranger had already disappeared into the woods.

"What did that person want?" Lucas asked as he caught his breath.

Grumblesnout raised his bushy white eyebrows and shook his head.

"Nothing, really," he said. "Just asked if I saw a shooting star last night."

Lucas and Clara glanced at each other. They were both thinking the same thing. *Maybe the shooting star and that stranger have something to do with the missing enderberries!*

"Let's go!" Lucas cried. "Thank you, Grumblesnout, and good-bye!"

As the troll waved farewell, they charged into the woods after the mysterious traveler.

CHAPTER 3

The Stranger

The children and Ruskin zigzagged between pine trees as they raced through the forest. Soon they came to a trail that spread out in three different directions. They looked from one trail to the next, but they couldn't tell which one the stranger had taken.

Lucas huffed and puffed. "It looks like our only clue just got away."

Clara put her hands on her knees to catch her breath. "I have another idea," she said. "Why don't we do some research in the royal library?"

Lucas thought for a moment. *Well, at least the library will get my*

mind off losing the stranger, he said to himself.

"Okay," he agreed. Then, with Ruskin leading the way, they tramped toward home. When they got to the castle, they hurried to the royal library.

The library had a whole section on trolls. Lucas and Clara each grabbed a book and sat on a bench topped with a purple velvet cushion. Ruskin curled up by their feet while they read.

"Here's something about enderberries!" said Clara excitedly.

Lucas looked up.

"Oh, never mind," she said. "It just says how much trolls like them."

She snapped the book shut and slid it back onto the shelf. Then she picked out another book and sat down. They both read quietly.

Suddenly Lucas's eyes grew wide.

Clara looked over. "Did you find something?" she asked.

Lucas nodded. "I found a legend about a pegasus," he said.

Clara leaned in closer. "You mean, like, a horse with wings?"

"Exactly," he said, pointing to a drawing on the page. "But what does a pegasus have to do with missing enderberries?"

Lucas couldn't take his eyes off the page. "It says here that a pegasus once visited Wrenly," he said. "And listen to this! It also says the pegasus loved the tart flavor of *enderberries.*"

"Let me see that!" said Clara as

she tugged at the edge of the book.

Lucas pulled it right back. "Hold your horses!" he said excitedly. "There's more!"

Lucas turned the page. Clara bounced on the cushion in suspense.

"It also says that the pegasus came down in a great ball of light!"

Clara's eyes widened.

"From its *floating castle in the sky*!" said Lucas triumphantly.

Clara suddenly made a frowny face. "You're making this up!" she declared.

Lucas stabbed the page with his

index finger. "It's all right here!" he said proudly.

Then he handed the book over to Clara. She reread the pages and saw for herself.

"Wow! Maybe it *is* true!" she said, mystified.

Lucas nodded knowingly. "That shooting star was headed straight for Burth," he said, "the land of enderberries!"

"Maybe the pegasus *has* returned to Wrenly," said Clara, believing it more and more every minute.

A wide grin spread over Lucas's face. "And it's our job to find it!"

CHAPTER 4
McGills'
Bakery

The Ghost Horse

The prince hitched two horses, Ivan and Scallop, to the rail outside the bakery. The children planned to get an early start, but first they had breakfast—warm blueberry muffins and milk. As they ate, they listened to Mr. Gills wait on a customer.

"Those are nice-looking horses you've got out there," said the customer, referring to Scallop and Ivan.

"One belongs to my daughter, Clara," Mr. Gills said proudly. "And the other to Prince Lucas."

The customer nodded and smiled.

"Speaking of horses," he went on, "I saw a very unusual one on the mainland yesterday. A white stallion stood in the foothills in the early-morning fog. It looked like a ghost horse. And then it *vanished* like a ghost too!"

Clara's father raised his eyebrows and looked at the man doubtfully.

"That *is* unusual," he commented.

"Yes . . . very unusual," repeated

the customer. Then he tucked his loaf of bread into a sack, tipped his hat, and headed for the door.

Clara pinched Lucas on the leg. "Are you thinking what I'm thinking?" she whispered.

Lucas nodded. "It might be the pegasus!"

"Let's get going," whispered Clara.

They packed some muffins and filled their canteens with water. Then they unhitched the horses and galloped across the mainland. When they got to the foothills, they began to look for clues.

Clara pointed to a print on the ground up ahead. "Is that something?" she wondered out loud.

The children studied the print. It looked like a horse hoofprint but with a twirling pattern. It was definitely some kind of animal track.

"The ground is soft from the rain we had the other day," Lucas observed. "So this might be a squishy pegasus track."

"There are more tracks up ahead," Clara said. "Let's see where they lead."

They followed the tracks into the forest. Ruskin wandered in front, sniffing the ground like a bloodhound. The tracks led to a clearing with a great oak tree in the middle.

Then the tracks ended just as mysteriously as they began.

"That's strange. The hoofprints end mid-stride," Lucas commented.

"You know what's even stranger?" Clara said under her breath. Lucas followed her gaze. There, on the edge of the clearing, stood the stranger they had seen the day before in Burth. This time her hood was down. It was a woman with short curly hair. The woman began to run toward Lucas and Clara. She swirled her lasso over her head.

"Get out of the way!" she cried.

Then everything happened at once. The branches above them began to shake. The stranger hurled her lasso into the tree. They heard the sound of thrashing wings in the treetop. Ruskin squawked nervously. Ivan and Scallop spooked, and the children had to fight to stay in their saddles.

WUMP!—the empty lasso fell to the ground with a thud.

Everything became quiet for a moment. Then a magnificent white stallion took flight from the tree. The creature had feathery silver-and-white angel wings, along with a golden tail and mane. Without a word, the woman ran off in the same direction as the pegasus.

Lucas and Clara both struggled to settle their frightened horses. But by the time the horses had quieted down, the female hunter and the pegasus were long gone.

CHAPTER 5

A Berry Good Idea

"We have to save the pegasus from that hunter!" declared Lucas.

"But how?" Clara asked.

A knowing smile swept across Lucas's face. "With enderberries!" he said.

Clara looked at the prince like he was crazy.

"Where are we going to get enderberries?" she questioned. "The trolls are already guarding what little they have left."

Lucas shrugged. "Maybe Cook knows where we can get some."

"Well, it's worth a try," said Clara doubtfully.

They galloped to the stables and returned the horses to their stalls. Then they hurried up the stone stairs and burst through the back door and into the kitchen. Cook jumped from his kettle in terror. His spoon clattered to the floor.

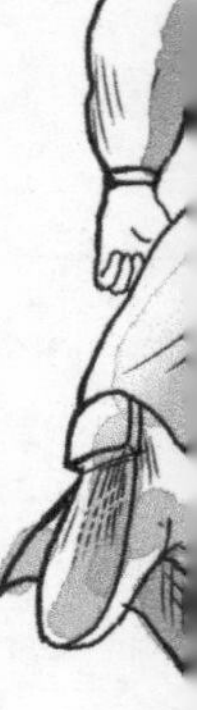

"Please don't do that ever again," he said, fanning himself with his

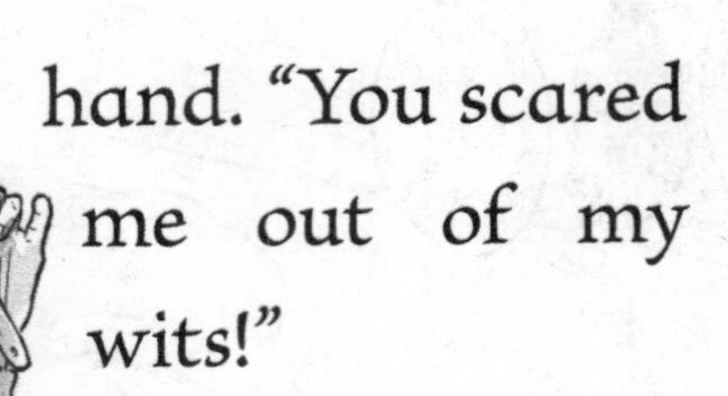

hand. “You scared me out of my wits!”

“We’re sorry,” said the prince, picking up Cook’s spoon.

“Everybody is always sorry,” complained Cook, cleaning his spoon on his apron. “Now, what is it I can do for you?”

“We wondered if you have any enderberries,” said Lucas.

Cook shook his head in surprise. “Enderberries!” he said dramatically.

"I do not prepare enderberries in *my* kitchen." He seemed a little bit offended.

"But do we *have* any?" Lucas persisted.

Cook let out a long sigh. "Yes, we have loads of enderberries!" he said. "The trolls give us those darn things every year as a gift! I don't have the heart to refuse them. Go ahead; help yourself. They're in the royal cupboard next to the raisins."

Lucas and Clara threw their arms around Cook. Then they thumped down the stairs to the royal cupboard and grabbed a basket of enderberries. They stowed it away in the playroom, behind the toy chest, for safekeeping. After the berries were hidden, Lucas saw Clara to the door.

"Okay, let's meet at the path to Mermaid's Cove at dusk," Lucas said.

"Don't forget the berries!" said Clara as she trotted down the lane toward home to help her father close up the shop.

CHAPTER 6

Dragon Talk

The children and Ruskin walked down the moonlit path to Mermaid's Cove. They crunched over the sand and looked for the perfect spot to watch for the pegasus. Lucas set the basket of enderberries out in the open. Then they hid in the shadow of a large rock and waited.

Soon Ruskin began to whine.

"Shhh," shushed Lucas.

The dragon swished his tail back and forth.

"I think he hears something," Clara whispered.

Lucas cupped his hand to his ear.

The faint sound of a ship's sail flapped in the wind. The sound

gradually grew louder. But it wasn't a ship's sail at all. It was the steady beat of pegasus wings! The snow-white stallion dropped to the sand and dipped his nose into the basket of enderberries. Ruskin let out a welcoming squawk. The pegasus looked

up and shook his mane calmly, as if to say hello in return.

"He's *so* beautiful," Clara said softly as she gazed at the velvety down feathers on the wings of the pegasus.

The pegasus twitched his ears at the sound of Clara's voice. He began to back away. Ruskin let out three short reassuring grunts and carefully walked over. The pegasus relaxed and returned to the basket of enderberries.

"Excellent work, Ruskin!" praised Lucas.

Ruskin squawked proudly.

"Can you ask the pegasus not to be afraid of us?" Clara whispered.

Ruskin nodded. Then he began to chirp, squawk, and grunt. The pegasus nickered and lowered his head. The great beast seemed to

understand that the children could be trusted. When the pegasus finished the enderberries, Lucas stepped forward.

"Why have you come to Wrenly?" he asked gently. Lucas noticed that the creature had

smudges of dirt and scratches on his body.

The animal shook his head. Ruskin then translated what the prince had said. The pegasus whinnied and lifted his head toward the great cloud in the sky—the same cloud

that had been hovering over Wrenly since the blue moon had begun. Ruskin whimpered understandingly.

"What did he say?" asked Lucas.

Ruskin loved to act things out for the children. First he pointed his muzzle toward the sky.

"The blue moon?" Clara guessed.

Ruskin shook his head no.

"The great cloud?" offered Lucas.

Ruskin nodded.

Then the dragon lifted his wing and let it flop to his side. He followed his action with a whimper.

“Your wing hurts?” Clara asked.

Ruskin shook his head and pointed at the pegasus.

“Oh, I get it!” Lucas said. “The pegasus has a hurt wing!”

“And he can’t fly back to his castle

in the sky!" said Clara, putting it all together.

Ruskin squawked in agreement.

Lucas walked up to the great winged stallion and stroked his face gently.

"Don't worry," he said softly. "We promise to take good care of you."

CHAPTER 7

The Stall

The children led the pegasus back to the royal stables.

"I'll talk with André and Grom first thing in the morning," said Lucas. André and Grom were the two finest wizards in Wrenly.

"But don't tell them we have the pegasus," warned Clara. "Then the whole kingdom will find out."

"Don't worry; I won't," said Lucas

reassuringly. “I’ll be clever. They will never suspect a thing.”

Clara looked relieved.

When they got near the stalls, Lucas went ahead to make sure no one was around.

“All clear,” he whispered upon his return. Then they walked the pegasus into an empty stall and covered him with a large wool blanket.

“Without your wings showing, you look like a regular horse,” Lucas declared. “And hopefully, the hunter won’t recognize you either.”

The pegasus blew air through his

nostrils. He seemed to like the safety of the enclosed stall.

"Well, I'd better be going before my parents get worried," Clara said. "I'll come back first thing in the morning."

Ruskin squawked.

"Shhh!" scolded Lucas.

Clara kneeled down and hugged Ruskin. "I'll see you in the morning too," she whispered.

The dragon crooned happily and curled up on

the straw beside the pegasus.

"Looks like Ruskin wants to stay the night," said Clara.

"Good thinking, Ruskin," Lucas said, patting his dragon on the head. "You can keep the pegasus company."

"And stay on the lookout!" added Clara.

Ruskin thumped his tail. Then the children headed for home.

The next morning Clara elbowed Lucas on the way to the stables.

"Look!" she hissed. "On the road up ahead!"

Lucas stopped in his tracks. It was the hunter, talking to the royal guards! The children ducked into the bushes. Then they crept along the inside of the hedge all the way to the stables.

"Phew!" Lucas said when he saw that the pegasus was still there.

"That was close," said Clara as she unhooked a bucket from the wall. "We'll have to work fast."

Then Clara crept outside to the trough to fill her bucket with water. Lucas got to work too. He examined the hurt pegasus's wing. The stallion winced.

"Sorry," whispered Lucas.

Clara's bucket of water sloshed as she carried it into the stall.

"I'll wash him and keep watch," she said. "You go talk to the wizards and see what you can find out."

Lucas gently lowered the hurt wing and turned to leave.

"Hurry," she whispered as she dipped a sponge in the water. "We don't have much time."

CHAPTER 8

Night Flight

Clara wiped her brow. The stall had become hot in the late-morning sun. Finally the door creaked open. Lucas had returned.

"What did you find out?" Clara asked.

Lucas patted the pegasus. "Not much," he said. "The wizards said time is the only thing that would heal a strained pegasus wing."

Clara groaned. "That's the one thing we *don't* have. That hunter is getting closer!"

Lucas looked at the poor pegasus thoughtfully. "Well, we'll just have to help the pegasus learn to fly with an injured wing."

They waited until after dark, and

then they snuck the pegasus out to an open field. The children massaged the pegasus's wing under the light of the blue moon. Then, on the count of three, the pegasus ran as fast as he could and took off in flight. The great stallion rose gracefully into

the starry night. Then he whinnied in pain and glided back down to the earth.

They tried again, but it was no use. The pegasus needed to heal before he could fly all the way home. Ruskin nuzzled the pegasus and stayed close to his side.

The children plopped down in the tall grass and listened to the crickets.

"Now what?" said Lucas.

But before Clara could respond, they heard something rustle in the woods nearby. Ruskin's ears perked up. The children stared into the darkness. A shadow emerged from the forest. It was the hunter!

Lucas and Clara scrambled to their feet and blocked the pegasus from the woman who gripped her lasso.

"Stay back!" Lucas ordered in a commanding voice.

But the stranger continued to walk toward them, into the moonlight. Suddenly the children could see her face. To their surprise, the stranger's eyes seemed to glow with kindness. She looked lovingly at the pegasus as if it were a long lost friend. The pegasus nickered and walked

past Lucas and Clara, right up to the stranger.

"I thought I'd never see you again!" the woman said gently, stroking his muzzle.

The pegasus whinnied softly.

"We don't have much time," said the stranger.

Lucas and Clara threw a curious glance at each other.

"We must get you home by tomorrow," the stranger said, "or else you will be trapped here, away from your family . . . forever."

CHAPTER 9

Grace

"Who are you?" asked Lucas, not knowing where else to begin.

The woman turned toward the children. "Oh, please forgive me," she said. "My name is Grace."

Clara took a step toward Grace. "And what do you want with the pegasus?" she asked.

Grace looked at the great cloud in the sky and then back at Clara.

"I want to help him get back to his homeland. When the blue moon is over, his castle in the sky will move on."

Lucas felt his shoulders relax.

"Phew," he said. "We thought you were a hunter."

"I am," she said. "But I hunt animals to help them—not harm them."

Ruskin squawked in approval.

"And I owe a great deal of thanks to you both," Grace went on. "How did you win the trust of the pegasus?"

Ruskin squawked again—only a little louder this time.

"Oh," Grace said to the dragon. "Did you have something to do with that?"

Lucas patted Ruskin on the back. "The pegasus seems to understand him," he said.

"What a good dragon," Grace said. Then she turned her attention

to the pegasus. She examined the stallion's wing in the moonlight.

"I knew something was wrong," she said, massaging the wing. "A pegasus often eats enderberries when it's in need of healing. Did you know that?"

The children shook their heads.

"Then," Grace continued, "when the trolls began to patrol the

enderberry bushes, the pegasus fled."

Lucas came closer. "But how do you know all this?" he asked.

Grace continued to massage the pegasus. "I met the pegasus once in a different kingdom," she said. "I became enchanted by this beautiful beast. After that, I studied everything there was to know about pegasi. When I saw the shooting star the other night, I knew a pegasus had returned. But I never dreamed it would be my same old friend."

"That is amazing," said Clara.

Grace smiled. "And now the

pegasus is in urgent need of more enderberries," she said. "Do you know where we can get some?"

Lucas nodded. "We have enderberries at the castle," he told her.

Grace sighed in relief. "That is good news," she said, smiling. "The pegasus needs rest first. Is there a safe place for him? He is a rare animal in this world, and there are many people who would cherish owning a pegasus."

"You can stay in the garden shed," suggested Lucas. "It's safe and quiet.

Plus Ruskin can stay with you. Clara and I will bring you the enderberries before dawn."

"That is a good plan," said Grace.

CHAPTER 10

The Salve

Early the next morning Lucas crept down the stairs to the larder while the rest of the castle slept. He helped himself to the last two baskets of enderberries. Then the prince slipped quietly out the kitchen door. Clara met him at the bottom of the steps. They each carried a basket.

The blue moon still shone in the sky as they walked across the empty

field. Clara spied a swirl of smoke streaming above the trees at the edge of the woods. Grace had built a fire and had set a kettle over the flame. The children placed the baskets of enderberries in front of Grace. She looked at them gratefully.

"Good morning," she said as she stirred the mixture.

"Good morning, Grace," Clara said. "What are you cooking?"

"It's called a salve," said Grace. "This will be a special potion to heal the pegasus."

Grace motioned to the enderberries. "Those are the most important part," she said, removing her spoon.

Grace added both baskets of enderberries into the kettle. The mixture bubbled, and the berries began to melt and pop in the hot liquid.

Grace kneeled and stirred in all

the berries. Then she let the mixture cook for an hour.

"The salve has to cool before we apply it," Grace said, removing the kettle from the fire.

Ruskin and the pegasus, who had just woken up, joined the group. They yawned and watched Grace tend to the other kettle.

"What are you making in that one?" asked Lucas.

"Breakfast," Grace said cheerfully. Breakfast sounded very good after a late night and a very early morning. The children got bowls and wooden spoons from the cabin. Grace heaped the bowls full of porridge. As they ate, the sun climbed higher into the sky.

"It is almost time," she said, keeping her eye on the sun. "When the sun peeks over the mountains, the castle will be revealed. That will be the pegasus's only chance to get home."

Lucas and Clara looked at the great cloud that still hung over Wrenly. The sun had nearly reached the top of the mountain.

Grace dipped her finger into the salve.

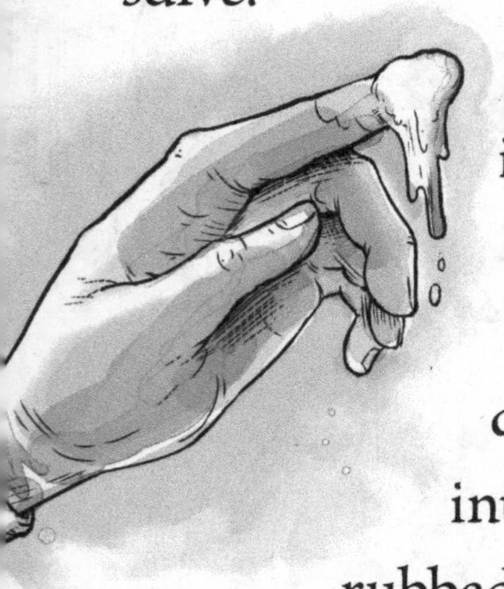

"It's still warm, but it's cool enough to be applied," she said.

Lucas and Clara dipped their hands into the salve and rubbed the mixture onto the pegasus's injured wing. They rubbed extra salve on the area where the

wing was attached to his body.

Grace, who had been keeping her eye on the sun, suddenly called out, "It's time!"

Lucas and Clara backed away from the beast carefully. Then the pegasus moved his great wings up and down. At the same time, something extraordinary happened. The great cloud over Wrenly moved away and revealed a grand, glistening castle in the sky.

Lucas whistled when he saw it. He had never seen anything so beautiful.

"It's now or never!" Grace cried.

The pegasus held his head high and whinnied to all his friends. Then he galloped toward the mountain, flapped his great wings, and lifted himself high up into the air. Ruskin squawked as he watched his new friend fly away. The pegasus neighed and then grew smaller and smaller in the distant sky. Finally, the winged creature landed safely on the craggy edge of the castle's land.

Rearing up on its hind legs one last time, the pegasus seemed to wave good-bye to his friends below.

The floating castle began to move on. The friends stood side by side and watched the castle and the blue moon slip over the horizon. They were quiet for a long time.

Then Lucas whispered, "Our wishes all came true."

Enter

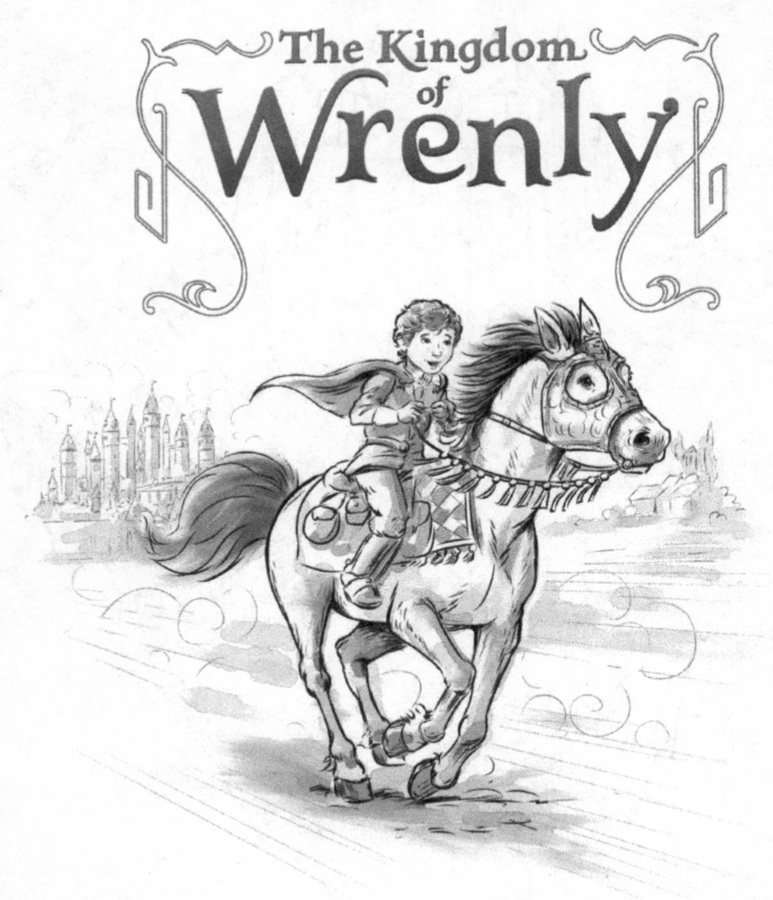

For more books, excerpts,
and activities, visit
KingdomofWrenly.com!